Winnie-the-Pooh
STORY TREASURY

"I wish to pay tribute to the work of E.H.Shepard
which has been inspirational in the creation of
these new drawings." *Andrew Grey*

EGMONT
We bring stories to life

This edition first published Great Britain in 2018
by Dean, an imprint of Egmont UK Limited
The Yellow Building, 1 Nicholas Road, London W11 4AN
Copyright © 2018 Disney Enterprises, Inc
Based on the 'Winnie-the-Pooh' works by A.A.Milne and E.H.Shepard
Illustrations by Andrew Grey

ISBN 978 0 6035 7664 5
70350/001
Printed in Malaysia

Egmont takes its responsibilites to the planet and its inhabitants very seriously.
We aim to use papers from well-managed forests run by responsible suppliers.

CONTENTS

Kanga

Winnie-the-Pooh

Owl

Piglet

Roo

Characters

Christopher
Robin

Eeyore

Rabbit

Tigger

Pooh Goes Visiting

Winnie-the-Pooh was walking through the Forest, humming proudly to himself. He had made up a little hum as he was doing his **Stoutness Exercises** in front of the glass:

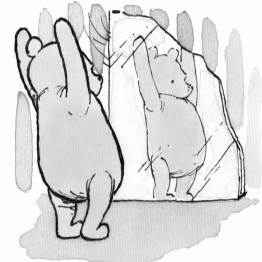

Tra-la-la, tra-la-la,

as he stretched up as high as he could go, and then

Tra-la-la, tra-la-la,

oh help! la,

as he tried to reach his toes.

After breakfast he had learnt it off by heart, and now he was humming it right through properly. It went like this:

Tra-la-la tra-la-la,
Tra-la-la, tra-la-la,
Rum-tum-tiddle-um-tum.
Tiddle-iddle, tiddle-iddle,
Tiddle-iddle, tiddle-iddle,
Rum-tum-tum-tiddle-um.

Pooh was humming this hum to himself, when suddenly he came to a sandy bank, and in the bank was a large hole.

"Aha!" said Pooh. (Rum-tum-tiddle-um-tum.) "If I know anything about anything, that hole means Rabbit and Rabbit means Company, and Company means Food and such like. Rum-tum-tum-tiddle-um."

So he bent down, put his head into the hole, and called out: "Is anybody at home?"

There was a sudden scuffling noise from inside the hole, and then silence.

"What I said was, 'Is anybody at home?'" called out Pooh very loudly.

"No!" said a voice; and then added, "You needn't shout, I heard you quite well the first time."

"Bother!" said Pooh. "Isn't there anybody here at all?"

"Nobody."

Pooh thought to himself, "There must be somebody there, because **somebody** must have said 'Nobody.'"

So he put his head back in the hole, and said, "Well, could you very kindly tell me where Rabbit is?"

"He has gone to see his friend Pooh Bear," said Rabbit.

"But this is **Me!**" said Pooh, very much surprised.

"Are you sure?" said Rabbit, still more surprised.

"Quite, quite sure," said Pooh.

"Oh, well then, come in."

So Pooh pushed

and pushed and pushed

his way through the hole, and at last he got in.

"You were quite right," said Rabbit, looking at him all ove

"It is you. Glad to see you."

"Who did you think it was?"

"Well, I wasn't sure. You know how it is in the Forest.

One can't have anybody coming into one's house. One has

to be careful. What about a mouthful of *something*?"

Pooh always liked a little *something* at eleven o'clock in the morning, and he was very glad to see Rabbit getting out the plates and mugs. When Rabbit said, "Honey or condensed milk with your bread?" he was so excited that he said, "Both," and then, so as not to seem greedy, he added, "But don't bother about the bread, please." And for a long time after that he said nothing.

At last, humming to himself in a rather sticky voice, Pooh got up, shook Rabbit lovingly by the paw, and said that he must be going on.

"Must you?" said Rabbit politely.

"Well," said Pooh, "I could stay a little longer if it – if you – and he tried very hard to look in the direction of the larder.

"As a matter of fact," said Rabbit, "I was going out myself directly."

"Oh well, then, I'll be going on. Goodbye."

"Well, goodbye, if you're sure you won't have any more."

"Is there any more?" asked Pooh quickly.

Rabbit took the covers off the dishes and said, "No, there isn't."

"I thought not," said Pooh, nodding to himself. "Well, goodbye. I must be going on."

So he started to climb out of the hole.

He **pulled** with his front paws,
and **pushed** with his back paws,
and in a little while his nose was
out in the open again . . . and
then his ears . . . and then his
front paws . . . and then his
shoulders . . . and then –

"Oh, help!" said Pooh.

"I'd better go back."

"Oh, bother!" said Pooh.

"I shall have to go on."

"I can't do either!" said Pooh.

"Oh, help and bother!"

Now, by this time Rabbit wanted to go for a walk too, and finding the front door **full**, he went out by the back door, and came round to Pooh, and looked at him.

"Hallo, are you stuck?" he asked.

"N-no," said Pooh carelessly. "Just resting and thinking and humming to myself."

"Here, give us a paw," said Rabbit.

Pooh Bear stretched out a paw, and Rabbit pulled and pulled and pulled . . .

"Ow!" cried Pooh. "You're hurting!"

"The fact is," said Rabbit, "you're stuck."

"It all comes," said Pooh crossly, "of not having front doors big enough."

"It all comes," said Rabbit sternly, "of eating too much. Well, well, I shall go and fetch Christopher Robin."

Christopher Robin lived at the other end of the Forest. When he came back with Rabbit, and saw the front half of Pooh sticking out of the hole, he said, "Silly old Bear," in such a loving voice that everybody felt quite hopeful again.

"I was just beginning to think," said Pooh, sniffing slightly, "that Rabbit might never be able to use his front door again. And I should hate that," he said.

"So should I," said Rabbit.

"Of course he'll use his front door again," said Christopher Robin.

"Good," said Rabbit.

"If we can't pull you out, Pooh, we might push you back."

Rabbit scratched his whiskers thoughtfully, and pointed out that when Pooh was pushed back, he was back –

"You mean I'd never get out?" said Pooh.

"I mean," said Rabbit, "that having got so far, it seems a pity to waste it."

Christopher Robin nodded.

"Then there's only one thing to be done," he said. "We shall have to wait for you to get thin again."

"How long does getting thin take?" asked Pooh anxiously.

"About a week, I should think," said Christopher Robin.

"But I can't stay here for a week!"

"You can stay here all right, silly old Bear.

It's getting you out which is so difficult."

"We'll read to you," said Rabbit cheerfully. "And I say, you're taking up a good deal of room in my house – do you mind if I use your back legs as a towel-rail? Because, I mean, there they are – doing nothing – and it would be very convenient just to hang the towels on them."

"A week!" said Pooh gloomily. "What about meals?"

"I'm afraid no meals," said Christopher Robin, "because of getting thin quicker. But we will read to you."

Pooh began to sigh, and then found he couldn't because he was so tightly stuck; and a tear rolled down his eye as he said: "Then would you read a Sustaining Book, such as would help and comfort a Wedged Bear in Great Tightness?"

So for a week Christopher Robin read that sort of book at the **North end** of Pooh, and Rabbit hung his washing on the **South end** . . . and in between, Pooh felt himself getting slenderer and slenderer.

Then at the end of the week Christopher Robin said, "Now!" And he took hold of Pooh's front paws while Rabbit took hold of Christopher Robin, and all Rabbit's friends and relations took hold of Rabbit, and they all pulled together...

And for a long time Pooh only said "Ow!"

And "Oh!"

And then, all of a sudden, he said:

"Pop!"

just as if a cork

were coming out of a bottle.

And Christopher Robin and Rabbit and all

Rabbit's friends and relations went **head-over-heels**

backwards . . . and on the top of them came

Winnie-the-Pooh – free.

So, with a nod of thanks to his friends, he went on with his walk through the forest, humming proudly to himself. Christopher Robin looked after him lovingly, and said to himself, "Silly old Bear!"

Piglet Meets a Heffalump

One day, Christopher Robin said carelessly:

"I saw a Heffalump today, Piglet."

"I saw one once," said Piglet. "At least I think I did."

"So **did I**," said Pooh, **wondering** what a Heffalump was like.

Then they talked about something else, until it was time for Pooh and Piglet to go **home.**

As they came to the Six Pine Trees, Pooh said: "Piglet, I have decided to catch a Heffalump." Pooh waited for Piglet to say "How?" but Piglet said nothing. The fact was Piglet was wishing that he had thought of it first.

"I shall do it," said Pooh, "by means of a Trap.

It must be a Cunning Trap, so you will have to help me, Piglet."

"How shall we do it?" said Piglet.

And they sat down to think it out.

Pooh's idea was that they should dig a Very Deep Pit, and the Heffalump would come and fall in.

"Why would he fall in?" said Piglet.

Pooh said the Heffalump might be looking up at the sky, wondering if it would rain, so he wouldn't see the Very Deep Pit until he was half-way down it.

Pooh felt sure that a bear with a **Very Clever Brain** could catch a Heffalump if he knew the **right way.**

"Suppose," he said to Piglet, "*you* wanted to catch *me*, how would you do it?"

"Well," said Piglet. "I should make a **Trap,** put a **Jar of Honey** in and you would **smell** it and go in after it, and –"

"And I should **lick** round the edges first and then the middle and then –" said Pooh **excitedly.**

"Yes, well never mind about that," said Piglet.

"The first thing to think of is, **What do Heffalumps like?** I should think haycorns, shouldn't you?"

Pooh, who had gone into a **happy dream**, woke with a start, and said **Honey** was a much more **trappy thing** than Haycorns.

"All right, *I'll* dig the pit, while *you* go and get the honey," said Piglet.

"Very well," said Pooh and he **stumped off.**

As soon as he got home, he took down a large jar from the top shelf. It had HUNNY written on it. He took a large lick. "Yes," he said, "it is. No doubt about that!" and he gave a deep sigh. Having made certain, he took the jar back to Piglet.

Piglet said, "Is that all you've got left?" and Pooh said, "Yes." Because it was. So Piglet put the jar at the bottom of the Pit and they went off home together.

"Good night," said Piglet. "And we meet at six o'clock tomorrow morning and see how many Heffalumps we've got in our Trap."

Some hours later, Pooh woke up. He was hungry.
He went to the larder, stood on a chair and reached
to the top shelf and found – nothing.

"That's funny," he thought. "I know I had a jar of honey
there. Then he began murmuring a murmur to himself:

It's very, very funny,
'cos I know I had some honey;
'cos it had a label on,
saying **HUNNY**

A goloptious full-up pot too,
And I don't know where it's gone to,
No, I don't know where it's gone
Well, it's funny.

Suddenly he remembered. He had put it into the **Cunning Trap.** He got back into bed but he couldn't sleep. He tried counting Heffalumps but every Heffalump was making **straight** for Pooh's honey, *and eating it all*. Pooh could bear it no longer. He jumped out of bed and ran to the Six Pine Trees.

In the half-light the **Very Deep Pit** seemed deeper. Pooh climbed in. "**Bother!**" said Pooh, as he got his nose inside the jar. "A Heffalump has been eating it!"

And then he thought a little and said, "Oh, no *I* **did.** I forgot." But there was a little left at the **very bottom** and he **pushed** his head right in, and began to **lick** . . .

By and by Piglet woke up. He **didn't** feel very brave. What was a Heffalump like? Was it **Fierce?** Wouldn't it be better to pretend he had a headache, and couldn't go to the Six Pine Trees? But suppose it was a very fine day, and there was no Heffalump in the Trap, here he would be, simply wasting his time for **nothing**. What should he do?

Then he had a Clever Idea. He would go now, peep into the Trap and see if there was a Heffalump there. If there was, he would go back to bed, and if there wasn't, he wouldn't. So off he went.

As he got nearer he could hear it heffalumping about like anything.

"Oh, dear, oh, dear, oh, dear!" said Piglet to himself. He wanted to run away but felt he must just see what a Heffalump was like. So he crept to the side of the Trap and looked in . . .

And all the time Winnie-the-Pooh had been trying to get the honey-jar off his head. He tried bumping it against things and tried to climb out of the Trap, but couldn't find his way. At last he lifted his head, jar and all, and made a roaring noise of Sadness and Despair . . . and it was at that moment that Piglet looked down.

"Help, help!" cried Piglet. "Horrible Heffalump!" and he scampered off as hard as he could. He didn't stop crying and scampering until he got to Christopher Robin's house.

"Whatever's the matter?" said Christopher Robin.

"Heff," said Piglet, "a Heff – a Heff – a Heffalump."

"What did it look like?"

"It had the biggest head you ever saw. A huge big – I don't know – like an enormous nothing. Like a jar."

"Well," said Christopher Robin, "I shall go and look at it. Come on."

"I can hear it, can't you?" said Piglet anxiously, as they got near.

"I can hear **something**," said Christopher Robin. It was Pooh bumping his head against a tree-root.

"There!" said Piglet. And he held on **tight** to Christopher Robin's hand.

Suddenly Christopher Robin began to laugh . . .
And while he was still laughing – Crash went the
Heffalump's head against the tree-root, Smash went
the jar, and out came Pooh's head again . . .

Then Piglet saw what a Foolish Piglet he had been, and he was so ashamed that he ran straight home and went to bed. Christopher Robin and Pooh went home to breakfast together.

"Oh, Bear!" said Christopher Robin.

"How I do **love** you!"

"So do I," said Pooh.

Eeyore Has a Birthday

Eeyore stood by the stream, and looked at himself in the water.

"Pathetic," he said. "That's what it is. Pathetic." He turned, splashed across the stream and turned to look at himself in the water again. "As I thought," he said. "No better from this side. But nobody cares."

There was a crackling noise in the bracken, and out came Pooh.

"Good morning, Eeyore," said Pooh.

"Good morning, Pooh Bear," said Eeyore, gloomily. "If it is a good morning, which I doubt."

"Oh!" said Pooh and he sat down on a large stone and sang Cottleston Pie for Eeyore:

Cottleston, Cottleston, Cottleston Pie,
A fly can't bird, but a bird can fly.
Ask me a riddle and I reply:
Cottleston, Cottleston, Cottleston Pie.

Cottleston, Cottleston, Cottleston Pie,
A fish can't whistle and neither can I.
Ask me a riddle and I reply:
Cottleston, Cottleston, Cottleston Pie.

Cottleston, Cottleston, Cottleston Pie,
Why does a chicken, I don't know why.
Ask me a riddle and I reply:
Cottleston, Cottleston, Cottleston Pie.

"That's right," said Eeyore. "Sing. Umty-tiddly, umpty-too. Enjoy yourself."

"I am," said Pooh. "But you seem so sad, Eeyore."

"Sad? Why should I be sad? It's my birthday. The happiest day of the year."

"Your birthday?" said Pooh, in great surprise.

"Of course it is. Can't you see? Look at all the presents I have had." He waved a foot from side to side.

Pooh looked – first to the right and then to the left. "Presents?" said Pooh. "Where? I can't see them!"

"Neither can I," said Eeyore. "Joke," he explained. "Ha, ha!"

Pooh scratched his head being a little puzzled. "But is it **really** your birthday?" he asked.

"It is."

"Oh! Well, **many happy returns** of the day, Eeyore."

"And many happy returns to you, Pooh Bear."

"But it isn't *my* birthday."

"No, it's mine."

"But you said 'Many happy returns' –"

"Well, why not? You don't want to be **miserable** on my birthday, do you?" said Eeyore. "It's bad enough being **miserable** myself, what with no presents and **no proper notice taken of me at all**, but if everybody else is going to be **miserable** too . . ."

This was **too much** for Pooh. "Stay there!" he called, as he hurried home; for he felt he must get Eeyore a **present** of some sort at once and he could always think of a proper one afterwards.

Outside his house, Pooh found Piglet jumping up and down trying to reach the knocker.

"What are you trying to do?" asked Pooh.

"I was trying to reach the knocker," said Piglet. "I just came round –"

"Let me do it for you," said Pooh, kindly. So he reached up and knocked at the door.

"I have just seen Eeyore," he began, "poor Eeyore is very Gloomy because it's his birthday, and nobody has taken any notice of it, and what a long time whoever lives here is taking to answer this door."

"But Pooh," said Piglet, "it's your own house!"

"Oh!" said Pooh. "So it is. Well, let's go in."

So in they went.

The first thing Pooh did was to go to the cupboard to see if he had quite a small jar of honey left. And he had, so he took it down.

"I'm giving this to Eeyore," he explained, "as a **present**. What are you going to give?"

"Couldn't I give it too?" said Piglet. "From **both** of us?"

"No," said Pooh. "That would not be a **good plan**."

"All right, then, I'll give him a **balloon**. I've got one left from my party. I'll go and get it now, shall I?" said Piglet.

"That, Piglet, is a **very good idea**. It is just what Eeyore wants to **cheer** him up. Nobody can be **un**cheered with a balloon."

So off Piglet trotted, and in the other direction went Pooh, with his jar of honey.

Pooh hadn't gone more than half-way when a sort of **funny feeling** began to creep all over him. It began at the tip of his nose and trickled all through him and out at the soles of his feet. It was just as if somebody inside him were saying, 'Now then, Pooh, time for a *little something.*'

So Pooh sat down to eat the honey.

As he took his last lick, he thought, "Now where was I going?" Then suddenly he remembered, he had eaten Eeyore's birthday present!

Then he thought: "Well, it's a very nice pot, and if I washed it clean, and got somebody to write 'A Happy Birthday' on it, Eeyore could keep things in it, which might be Useful."

As Pooh was passing the Hundred Acre Wood, he went
to call on Owl, who lived there.

"Many happy returns of Eeyore's birthday," said Pooh. "I'm giving Eeyore a **Useful Pot** to keep things in, and I wanted to ask you –"

Owl looked at the pot. "You ought to write 'A Happy Birthday' on it," he added.

"That was what I wanted to ask you," said Pooh. "Because my spelling is **Wobbly** and the letters get in the wrong places. Would you write 'A Happy Birthday' on it for me?"

"Can you read, Pooh?" Owl asked, a little anxiously. "There's a notice about knocking and ringing outside my door, which Christopher Robin wrote. Could you read it?"

"Christopher Robin told me what it said, and then I could," said Pooh.

"Well, I'll tell you what this says, and then you'll be able to," said Owl.

This is what Owl wrote:

HIPY PAPY BTHUTHDTH THUTHDA BTHUTHDY.

"I'm just saying 'A Happy Birthday'," said Owl, nervously.

"It's a nice long one," said Pooh, very much impressed by it.

"Well, actually, of course, I'm saying 'A very Happy Birthday with love from Pooh.'"

While all this was happening, Piglet had gone back to his house to get Eeyore's balloon. He held it **tightly** against himself so it shouldn't **blow away,** and ran as fast as he could to get to Eeyore before Pooh so he would be the **first one** to give a present. And running along, thinking how pleased Eeyore would be, he tripped on a rabbit hole, and fell flat on his face.

"BANG!!!!???!!!

Piglet wondered what had happened.

Had the Forest blown up?

Or had he and was he now alone on the moon

or somewhere?

Piglet got up.

He was still

in the

Forest!

"That's funny,"

he thought.

"I wonder what that bang was. And where's my

balloon? And what's that small piece of damp rag?"

It was the balloon!

"Oh, dear!" said Piglet. "Oh, dearie, dearie, dear!

I can't go back, and I haven't another balloon. Perhaps

Eeyore doesn't like balloons so very much."

So he trotted on, rather sadly now, and soon reached

Eeyore at the stream.

"Many happy returns of the day," said Piglet, having now got closer.

Eeyore stopped looking at himself in the stream, and turned to stare at Piglet.

"Just say that again," he said, as he balanced on three legs, bringing his fourth leg up to his ear. He pushed his ear forward with his hoof.

"Many happy returns of the day," said Piglet, again.

"My birthday?" said Eeyore.

"Yes, Eeyore, and I've brought you a present. A balloon."

"Balloon?" said Eeyore. "One of those big coloured things you blow up?"

"Yes, but I'm very sorry, Eeyore – I fell down."

"Dear, how unlucky! You didn't hurt yourself, Little Piglet?"

"No, but I – I – oh, Eeyore, I burst the balloon!"

There was a very long silence.

"My balloon?" said Eeyore at last.

Piglet nodded. "Yes, Eeyore," said Piglet, sniffing a little. "Here it is. With – with many happy returns of the day."

And he gave Eeyore the small piece of damp rag.

"Is this it?" said Eeyore, a little surprised. "My present?"

Piglet nodded again.

"Thank you, Piglet," said Eeyore. "What colour was it when it – when it was a **balloon**?"

"Red."

"My **favourite** colour," said Eeyore, thoughtfully. "Well, well."

Piglet felt very miserable, and didn't know what to say.

Suddenly, there was Pooh.

"Many happy returns of the day," said Pooh.

"Thank you, Pooh, I'm having them," said Eeyore, gloomily.

"I've brought you a little present," said Pooh, excitedly. "It's a **Useful Pot**," said Pooh. "And it's got 'A Very Happy Birthday with love from Pooh' written on it. And it's for putting things in. There!"

When Eeyore saw the pot, he was quite excited. "I believe my Balloon will go into that Pot!"

"Oh, no, Eeyore," said Pooh. "Balloons are much too big to go into Pots."

"Not mine," said Eeyore proudly. "Look, Piglet!" And as Piglet looked sadly round, Eeyore placed the balloon carefully in the pot.

"So it does!" said Pooh. "It goes in!"

"So it does!" said Piglet. "And it comes out!"

"Doesn't it?" said Eeyore. "It goes in and out like anything."

"I'm very glad," said Pooh, "that I thought of giving you a **Useful Pot** to put things in."

"I'm very glad," said Piglet, "that I thought of giving you Something to put in a Useful Pot."

But Eeyore wasn't listening. He was taking the balloon out, and putting it back again, as happy as could be.

Piglet Has a Bath

Nobody seemed to know where they came from, but there they were in the Forest: Kanga and Baby Roo.

Pooh asked Christopher Robin, "How did they come here?"

Christopher Robin said, "In the Usual Way, if you know what I mean, Pooh."

And Pooh said, "Ah!" Then he went to call upon Piglet to see what he thought and at Piglet's house he found Rabbit, so they all talked about it.

"What I don't like about it is this," said Rabbit. "Here are we, all of us, and then suddenly, we wake up one morning, and what do we find? We find a Strange animal among us. An animal who carries her family about with her in her pocket!"

"The question is," said Piglet, "what are we to do about Kanga?"

"The best way," said Rabbit, "would be this. Hide Baby Roo and then when Kanga says, 'Where's Baby Roo?' we say, 'Aha!'"

"Aha!" said Pooh, practising.

"We say 'Aha!'" said Rabbit, "so Kanga knows that we know where Baby Roo is. 'Aha!' means 'We'll tell you where Roo is, if you promise to go away and never come back to the Forest.'"

"There's just one thing," said Piglet, fidgeting a bit. "Christopher Robin said a Kanga was Generally Regarded as One of the Fiercer Animals. And it is well known that if One of the Fiercer Animals is Deprived of Its Young, it becomes as fierce as Two of the Fiercer Animals. In which case 'Aha!' is perhaps a foolish thing to say!"

"Piglet," said Rabbit, "you haven't any pluck."

"It is hard to be brave," said Piglet, sniffing slightly, "when you're only a Very Small Animal."

Rabbit, who had begun to write very busily, looked up and said: "It is because you are a Very Small Animal that you will

be Useful in the adventure before us."
Piglet was so excited at the idea of being Useful that the forgot to be frightened.

"What about me?" said Pooh sadly. "I suppose I shan't be useful?"

"Never mind, Pooh," said Piglet comfortingly.

"Without Pooh," said Rabbit solemnly, "the adventure would be impossible."

"Oh!" said Piglet, and tried not to look disappointed. Pooh went into a corner of the room and said proudly to himself, "Impossible without Me! That sort of Bear."

"Now listen all of you," said Rabbit, when he had finished writing, and Pooh and Piglet sat listening very eagerly.

This was what Rabbit read out:

PLAN tO CAPTURE BABY ROO

1 General Remarks. Kanga runs faster than any of Us, even Me.

2 More General Remarks. Kanga never takes her eye off Baby Roo, except when he's safely buttoned up in her pocket.

3 Therefore. If we are to Capture Baby Roo, we must get a Long Start, because Kanga runs faster than any of Us, even Me. (See 1.)

4 A Thought. If Roo had jumped out of Kanga's pocket and Piglet had jumped in, Kanga wouldn't know the difference, because Piglet is a Very Small Animal.

5 Like Roo.

6 But Kanga would have to be looking the other way first, so as not to see Piglet jumping in.

7 See 2.

8 Another Thought. But if Pooh was talking to her very excitedly, she might look the other way for a moment.

9 And then I could run away with Roo.

10 Quickly.

11 And Kanga wouldn't discover the difference until Afterwards.

Rabbit

For a little while nobody said anything. And then Piglet said: "And – Afterwards? When Kanga does

Discover the Difference?"

"Then we all say 'Aha!' Why, what's the trouble, Piglet?" said Rabbit.

"Nothing," said Piglet, "as long as we all three say it. I shouldn't care to say 'Aha!' by myself. It wouldn't sound nearly so well."

"Well, Pooh?" said Rabbit. "You see what you have to do?"

"No," said Pooh Bear. "Not yet," he said.

"What do I do?"

"You just have to talk **very hard** to Kanga so as she doesn't notice anything."

"Oh! What about?"

"Anything you like."

"You mean like telling her a little bit of poetry or something?"

"That's it," said Rabbit. "Splendid. Now come along."

So they all went out to look for Kanga.

Kanga and Roo were in a sandy part of the Forest. Baby Roo was practising very small jumps in the sand, and falling down mouse-holes and climbing out of them. Kanga was saying, "Just one more jump, dear, and then we must go home."

And at that moment who should come stumping up the hill, but Pooh.

"Good afternoon, Kanga."

"Good afternoon, Pooh."

"We were just going home," said Kanga. "Good afternoon, Rabbit. Good afternoon, Piglet."

Rabbit and Piglet, who had come up from the other side of the hill, said "Good afternoon," and Roo asked them to look at him jumping, so they stayed and looked.

"Oh, Kanga," said Pooh, after Rabbit had winked at him twice, "I don't know if you are interested in Poetry at all?"

"Hardly at all," said Kanga.

"Oh!" said Pooh.

"Go on," said Rabbit, in a **loud whisper** behind his paw.

"Talking of Poetry," said Pooh, "I made up a little piece as I was coming along. It went like this. Er – now let me see –"

"You must listen **very carefully**," said Rabbit to Kanga.

"So as not to miss any of it," said Piglet.

"Oh, yes," said Kanga, but she still looked at Baby Roo.

Pooh gave a little cough and began.

LINES WRITTEN BY
A BEAR OF VERY LITTLE BRAIN

On Monday, when the sun is hot
I wonder to myself a lot:
"Now is it true, or is it not,
That what is which and which is what?"

On Tuesday, when it hails and snows,
The feeling on me grows and grows
That hardly anybody knows
If those are these or these are those.

On Wednesday, when the sky is blue,
And I have nothing else to do,
I sometimes wonder if it's true
That who is what and what is who.

On Thursday, when it starts to freeze
And hoar-frost twinkles on the trees,
How very readily one sees
That these are whose - but whose are these?

On Friday -

"Yes, it is, isn't it?" said Kanga, not waiting to hear what happened on Friday. "Just one more jump, Roo, dear, and then we **really** must be going."

"Talking of Poetry," said Pooh quickly, "have you ever noticed that tree right over there?"

"No," said Kanga. "Jump in, Roo, dear, and we'll go home."

"You ought to look at that tree right over there," said Rabbit. "Shall I lift you in, Roo?" And he picked up Roo in his paws.

"I can see a bird in it from here," said Pooh. "Or is it a fish?"

"It isn't a fish, it's a bird," said Piglet.

"So it is," said Rabbit.

And then at last Kanga did turn her head to look. And the moment that her head was turned, Rabbit said in a loud voice "In you go, Roo!" and in jumped Piglet into Kanga's pocket, and off scampered Rabbit, with Roo in his paws, as fast as he could.

"Are you all right, Roo, dear?" said Kanga.

Piglet made a squeaky Roo-noise from the bottom of Kanga's pocket.

"Rabbit had to go away," said Pooh. "I think he thought of something he had to go and see about suddenly."

"And Piglet?"

"I think Piglet thought of something at the same time. **Suddenly**."

"Well, we must be getting home," said Kanga.

"Goodbye, Pooh."

And in **three large jumps** she was gone.

Pooh looked after her as she went.

"I wish I could jump like that," he thought. "Some can and some can't. That's how it is."

But there were moments when Piglet wished that Kanga **couldn't**. Often, when he had had a long walk home through the Forest, he had wished that he were a bird; but now he thought jerkily to himself at the bottom of Kanga's pocket, "If this is flying I shall never really take to it." And he was saying,

all the way to Kanga's house.

Of course as soon as Kanga unbuttoned her pocket, she saw what had happened. For a moment she was **frightened**, and then she knew she wasn't; for she felt sure that Christopher Robin would never let any harm happen to Roo. So she said to herself, "If they are having a joke with me, I will have a joke with them."

"Now then, Roo, dear," she said, as she took Piglet out of her pocket. "Bedtime."

"Aha!" said Piglet, as well as he could after his **Terrifying Journey**. But it wasn't a very good "Aha!" and Kanga didn't seem to understand what it meant.

"Bath first," said Kanga in a cheerful voice. Piglet looked round for the others. But the **others** weren't there!

Rabbit was playing with Baby Roo in his own house, and feeling more **fond** of him every minute,

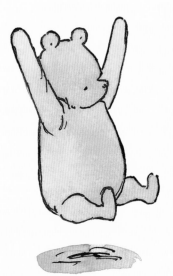

and Pooh, who had decided to be a Kanga, was **still** at the sandy place at the top of the Forest, practising jumps.

"I wonder," said Kanga, "if it would be a good idea to have a **cold bath** this evening. Would you like that, Roo, dear?"

Piglet had never been really fond of baths, so in as brave a voice as he could he said:

"Kanga, **I am not Roo**, I am Piglet!"

"Yes, dear, yes," said Kanga, soothingly. "And imitating Piglet's voice too! **So clever** of you," she went on, as she took a **large** bar of soap out of the cupboard.

"Can't you see?" shouted Piglet. "Haven't you got eyes? Look at me!"

"I am looking, Roo, dear," said Kanga rather severely.

"And if you go on making faces like Piglet's, you will grow up to look like Piglet – and then think how sorry you will be. Now then, into the bath, and don't let me have to speak to you about it again."

Before he knew where he was, Piglet was in the bath, and Kanga was scrubbing him firmly with a large lathery flannel.

"Ow!" cried Piglet. "Let me out! I'm Piglet!"

"Don't open the mouth, dear, or the soap goes in," said Kanga. "There! What did I tell you?"

"You – you – you did it on purpose," spluttered Piglet, as soon as he could speak again.

"That's right, dear, don't say anything," said Kanga, and in another minute Piglet was out of the bath, and being rubbed dry with a towel.

"Now," said Kanga, "there's your **medicine**, and then bed."

"W-w-what medicine?" said Piglet.

"To make you grow **big and strong**, dear. You don't want to grow up small and weak like Piglet, do you? Well, then!"

At that moment there was a knock at the door.

"Come in," said Kanga, and in came Christopher Robin.

"Christopher Robin!" cried Piglet. "Tell Kanga who I am! She keeps saying I'm Roo. I'm not Roo, am I?"

Christopher Robin looked at him **very carefully**, and shook his head.

"You can't be Roo," he said, "because I've just seen Roo playing in Rabbit's house."

"There you are!" said Piglet. "I told you so. **I'm Piglet.**"

Christopher Robin shook his head again.

"**Oh, you're not Piglet**," he said. "I know Piglet well, and he's quite a **different colour**."

Piglet began to say that this was because he had just had a bath, and as he opened his mouth, Kanga slipped the medicine spoon in and patted him on the back.

"I knew it wasn't Piglet," said Kanga. "I wonder who it can be?"

"Perhaps it's some relation of Pooh's," said Christopher Robin.

Kanga agreed this was probably what it was, and said that they would have to call it by some name.

"I shall call it Pootel," said Christopher Robin. "Henry Pootel for short."

And just when this was decided, Henry Pootel wriggled out of Kanga's arms and ran to the open door. Never had Henry Pootel Piglet run so fast as he ran then. He didn't stop running until he had got quite close to his house. But when he was a hundred yards away, he stopped running and

 rolled the rest

of the way home,

to get his own nice

comfortable colour again.

So Kanga and Roo stayed in the Forest. And every Tuesday Roo spent the day with his great friend Rabbit, and every Tuesday Kanga spent the day teaching her great friend Pooh to jump, and every Tuesday Piglet spent the day with his great friend Christopher Robin. So they were all happy again.

Pooh Builds a House

One day when Pooh Bear had nothing else to do, he went round to Piglet's house to see what Piglet was doing. But to his surprise he saw that the door was open, and the more he looked inside the more Piglet wasn't there.

He thought that he would knock very loudly just to make quite sure . . . and while he waited, a hum came suddenly into his head . . .

The more it snows
(Tiddely pom),
The more it goes
(Tiddely pom),
The more it goes
(Tiddely pom),
On Snowing.
And nobody knows
(Tiddely pom),
How cold my toes
(Tiddely pom),
How cold my toes
(Tiddely pom),
Are growing.

"So what I'll do," said Pooh, "is I'll just go home first and see what the time is, and then I'll go and see Eeyore and sing it to him."

He hurried back to his own house, and when he suddenly saw Piglet sitting in his best armchair, he could only stand there wondering whose house he was in.

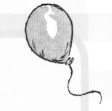

"Hallo, Piglet," he said. "I thought you were out."

"No," said Piglet, "it's you who were out, Pooh."

"So it was," said Pooh. "I knew one of us was."

"Nearly eleven o'clock," said Pooh, happily. "You're just in time for a little **smackerel of something**, and then we'll go out and sing my song to Eeyore."

"Which song, Pooh?" asked Piglet.

"The one we're going to sing to Eeyore," explained Pooh.

Half an hour later, Pooh and Piglet set out on their way.

In a little while, Piglet was feeling more snowy behind the ears than he had ever felt before.

"Pooh," he said, a little timidly, because he didn't want Pooh to think he was Giving In. "I was just wondering. How would it be if we went home now and practised your song, and then sang it to Eeyore tomorrow?"

"It's no good going home to practise it," said Pooh, "because it's a special Outdoor Song which Has To Be Sung In The Snow. We'll practise it now as we go along."

By this time they were getting near Eeyore's Gloomy Place.

"I've been thinking," said Pooh, "poor Eeyore has nowhere to live. So what I've been thinking is this. Let's build him a house."

"That," said Piglet, "is a Grand Idea. Where shall we build it?"

"We will build it here," said Pooh. "And we will call this Pooh Corner."

"I saw a heap of sticks on the other side of the wood," said Piglet.

"Thank you, Piglet," said Pooh. "What you have just said will be a **Great Help** to us."

And they went round to the other side of the wood to fetch the sticks.

Christopher Robin had spent the morning indoors and was just wondering what it was like OUTSIDE, when who should come knocking but Eeyore.

"Hallo, Eeyore," said Christopher Robin. "How are *you*?"

"I suppose you haven't seen a house or what-not anywhere about?" said Eeyore.

"Who lives there?" asked Christopher Robin.

"I do. At least I thought I did. But I suppose I don't. After all, we can't all have houses," Eeyore replied.

"Oh, Eeyore!" said Christopher Robin, feeling very sorry.

"I don't know how it is, Christopher Robin," continued Eeyore, "but what with all this snow and one thing and another,

it isn't so Hot in my field about three o'clock in the morning as some people think it is. In fact,

Christopher Robin," he went on in a loud whisper, "quite-between-ourselves-and-don't-tell-anybody, it's Cold."

"Oh, Eeyore!" said Christopher Robin again.

"So what it all comes down to is that I built myself a **house** down by my little wood," said Eeyore, in his most melancholy voice. "But when I came home today, it wasn't there."

"We'll go and look for it at once," said Christopher Robin.

And off they **hurried**, and in a very little time they got to the corner of the field where Eeyore's house wasn't any longer.

"There!" said Eeyore. "Not a **stick** of it left! Of course, I've still got **all this snow** to do what I like with. One mustn't complain."

But Christopher Robin wasn't listening to Eeyore, he was listening to **something else**.

"We've finished our HOUSE!"

sang a gruff voice.

"Tiddely pom!"

sang a squeaky one.

"It's a beautiful HOUSE . . ."

"Tiddely pom . . ."

"I wish it were MINE . . ."

"Tiddely pom . . ."

"Pooh!" shouted Christopher Robin.

The singers stopped suddenly. "It's Christopher Robin!" said Pooh eagerly.

"He's round by the place where we got all those sticks from," said Piglet.

And they hurried round the corner of the wood, Pooh making **welcoming noises** all the way.

When Christopher Robin had given Pooh a hug, he began to explain the sad story of Eeyore's Lost House. And Pooh and Piglet listened, and their eyes seemed to get bigger and bigger.

"*Where* did you say it was?" asked Pooh.

"Just here," said Eeyore.

"Made of sticks?"

"Yes."

"Oh!" said Piglet, nervously. And so as to seem quite at ease he hummed tiddely-pom once or twice in a **what-shall-we-do-now** kind of way.

"The fact is," said Pooh. "Well, the fact is . . ."
and he nudged Piglet.

"It's like this . . ." said Piglet. "Only **warmer**,"
he added, after deep thought.

"What's **warmer?**"

"The other side of the wood, where Eeyore's
house is," said Piglet.

"*My* house?" said Eeyore. "My house was here."

"No," said Piglet, firmly. "The other side of the wood."

"Because of being warmer," said Pooh.

"Come and look," said Piglet simply, and he led the way.

They came round the corner and there was Eeyore's house, looking as comfy as anything. Eeyore went inside . . . and came out again.

"It is my house," he said. "And I built it where I said I did, so the wind must have blown it here. And here it is as good as ever. In fact, better in places."

"Much better," said Pooh and Piglet together. So they left him in it.

Christopher Robin went back to lunch with his friends Pooh and Piglet, and on the way they told him of the **Awful Mistake** they had made. And when he had finished laughing, they all sang the **Outdoor Song** for Snowy Weather the rest of the way home. Piglet, who was still not quite sure of his voice, putting in the **tiddely-poms** again.

"And I know it *seems* easy," said Piglet to himself,

"but it isn't *everyone* who could do it."

Pooh Invents a New Game

One day, Pooh was walking through the Forest, trying to make up a piece of poetry about **fir-cones**. He picked one up, then this came into his head **suddenly**:

Here is a myst'ry
About a little fir-tree.
Owl says it's his tree,
And Kanga says it's her tree.

He had just reached a bridge and, not looking where he was going, he **tripped** and the fir-cone jerked out of his paw into the river.

"Bother," said Pooh, as he lay down to watch the river. Suddenly, there was his fir-cone.

"That's funny," said Pooh. "I dropped it on the other side and it came out on this side! I wonder if it would do it again?" And he went back for some more fir-cones.

It did. It kept on doing it. Then he dropped one **big one** and one little one, and the big one came out first, which was what he had said it would do, and the little one came out last, which was what he had said it would do. So he had won twice.

And that was the beginning of the game called **Poohsticks**, that Pooh and his friends used to play with **sticks** instead of fir-cones, because they were easier to mark.

One day, Pooh and Piglet and Rabbit and Roo were playing Poohsticks. They had dropped their sticks in when Rabbit said "Go!" and then hurried to the other side of the bridge to see whose stick would come out first.

"I can see mine!" cried Roo. "No, I can't! It's **something else.** Can you see yours, Pooh?"

"No," said Pooh.

"I expect my stick's stuck," said Roo.

"They always take longer than you think," said Rabbit.

"I can see yours, Piglet," said Pooh, **suddenly**. "It's coming over to my side."

Piglet got **very excited** because his was the only one that had been seen, and that meant **he was winning**.

"Are you sure it's mine?" he squeaked, excitedly.
"Yes, because it's grey. Here it comes! A very . . .
big . . . grey . . . oh, no, it isn't, it's Eeyore."

And

out

floated

Eeyore.

"Eeyore, what *are* you doing there?" said Rabbit.

"I'll give you three guesses, Rabbit," said Eeyore. "Digging holes in the ground? Wrong. Leaping from branch to branch of a tree? Wrong. Waiting for somebody to help me out of the river? Right."

"But, Eeyore," said Pooh, "what can we . . . I mean, how shall we . . . do you think if we . . ."

"Yes," said Eeyore. "One of those would be just the thing. Thank you, Pooh."

"I've got a **sort of idea**," said Pooh at last, "but I don't suppose it's a very good one."

"Go on, Pooh," said Rabbit.

"Well, if we **threw stones** into the river on *one* side of Eeyore, the stones would **make waves**, and the waves would **wash him** to the other side."

Pooh got a **big stone** and leant over the bridge. "I'm not throwing it, I'm **dropping it**, Eeyore," he explained. "And then I can't miss – I mean I can't hit you."

Pooh dropped his stone. There was a **loud splash**, and Eeyore **disappeared.**

It was an anxious moment for the watchers on the
bridge. Then something grey showed for a moment
by the river bank. It slowly got bigger and bigger
and at last it was Eeyore coming out. With a shout they
rushed off the bridge.

"Well done, Pooh," said Rabbit, kindly. "That was a good idea, hooshing Eeyore to the bank like that."

"Hooshing me?" said Eeyore, in surprise. "Pooh dropped a large stone on me, and so as not to be struck heavily on the chest, I dived and swam to the bank."

"How did you **fall in**, Eeyore?" asked Rabbit.

"Somebody **bounced** me. I was just thinking by the side of the river, when I received a loud **bounce**," said Eeyore.

"But who did it?" asked Roo.

"I expect it was **Tigger**," said Piglet, nervously.

There was a **loud noise** behind them, and through the hedge came **Tigger** himself.

"Hallo, everybody," said Tigger, cheerfully.

Rabbit became very important suddenly.

"Tigger," he said. "What happened just now?"

"Just when?" said Tigger.

"When you bounced Eeyore into the river."

"I didn't bounce him. I had a cough, and said,

grrrr oppp ptschschschz!"

158

"That's what I call **bouncing**," said Eeyore. "Taking people **by surprise**."

"I didn't **bounce**, I coughed," said Tigger, **crossly**. "**Bouncy** or Coffy, it's all the same at the **bottom** of the river," said Eeyore.

Christopher Robin came down to the bridge and saw all the animals there.

"It's like this, Christopher Robin," began Rabbit. "Tigger –"

"All I did was I coughed," said Tigger.

"He bounced," said Eeyore.

"Well, I sort of boffed," said Tigger.

"Hush!" said Rabbit. "What does Christopher Robin think about it all? That's the point."

"Well," said Christopher Robin, not quite sure what it was all about. "I think we all ought to play Poohsticks."

So they did. And Eeyore, who had never played it before, won more times than anybody else; and Roo fell in twice, the first time by accident and the second time on purpose, because he saw Kanga coming and knew he'd have to go to bed anyhow.

So then Rabbit said **he'd go** with them; and
Tigger and Eeyore **went off** together. Christopher
Robin and Pooh and Piglet were left on the bridge
by themselves.

For a long time they looked at the river beneath them, **saying nothing,** and the river said nothing too, for it felt very quiet and peaceful on this summer afternoon.

"Tigger is all right, *really*," said Piglet, lazily.

"Of course he is," said Christopher Robin.

"Everybody is *really*," said Pooh. "That's what *I* think, but I don't suppose I'm **right**."

"Of course you are," said Christopher Robin.

Tigger is Unbounced

One hot summer's day, Rabbit was talking to Pooh and Piglet. Pooh wasn't really listening. From time to time, he opened his eyes to say, "Ah!"

Rabbit said, "You see what I mean, Piglet," and Piglet nodded to show that he did.

"In fact," said Rabbit, "Tigger's getting so bouncy nowadays that it's time we taught him a lesson. Don't you think so, Piglet?"

Piglet agreed Tigger was very **bouncy** and if they could think of a way of unbouncing him, it would be a **Very Good Idea**.

"What do *you* say, Pooh?" asked Rabbit.

Pooh opened his eyes and said, "Extremely."

"Extremely what?" asked Rabbit.

"What you were saying," said Pooh. "Undoubtably."

"But how shall we do it?" asked Piglet. "What sort of a lesson?"

"That's the point," said Rabbit.

"What were we talking about?" asked Pooh.

Piglet explained that they were trying to think of a way to get the bounces out of Tigger, because however much you liked him, you couldn't deny it, he did bounce.

"Oh, I see," said Pooh. He tried to think, but he could only think of something which didn't help at all.

So he hummed it very quietly to himself.

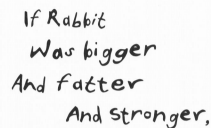

If Rabbit
Was bigger
And fatter
And stronger,

or bigger
Than Tigger,

If Tigger was smaller,

Then Tigger's bad habit
Of bouncing at Rabbit

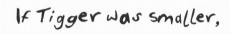

Would matter
No longer,

If Rabbit
Was taller.

"I've an idea!" said Rabbit. "We take Tigger for a **long explore** and we lose him. The next morning we find him again and he'll be a **different Tigger** altogether. He'll be a Humble Tigger,

a Sad Tigger,

a Melancholy Tigger,

a Small and Sorry Tigger,

an Oh-Rabbit-I-am-glad-to-see-you Tigger.

That's why."

"I should hate him to go on being Sad," said Piglet.

"Tiggers never go on being Sad," explained Rabbit. "But if we can make Tigger feel Small and Sad just for **five minutes**, we shall have done a **good deed**."

So the only question was, where should they lose Tigger?

"We'll take him to the North Pole," said Rabbit.
"It was a long explore finding it, so it will be a
very long explore for Tigger un-finding it again."

Pooh felt glad. It was he who had first found the
North Pole so when they got there, Tigger would see
a notice saying,

and Tigger would then know what sort of bear he
was. That sort of bear. So it was arranged that they
would start the next morning and Rabbit would go
and ask Tigger to come.

The next day was quite a different day. Instead of being sunny, it was **cold** and **misty**. Pooh felt sorry for the bees who wouldn't be making honey on such a day.

Piglet wasn't thinking of that, but of how **cold** and **miserable** it would be being lost **all day** and **night** on top of the Forest on such a day.

Rabbit said it was just the day for them. As soon as Tigger bounced out of sight, they would hurry in the other direction, and he would never see them again.

"Not never?" said Piglet, worriedly.

"Well, not until we find him again," said Rabbit. "Come on. He's waiting for us."

At Kanga's house, they found Roo waiting for them too. This made things Very Awkward. Rabbit whispered behind his paw to Pooh, "Leave this to me!"

"Roo had better not come today," he said to Kanga. "He was coughing earlier."

"Oh Roo, you never told me," said Kanga, reproachfully.

"It was a biscuit cough," said Roo. "Not one you tell about."

"I think not today, dear. Another day," Kanga said.

"Ah, Tigger! There you are!" said Rabbit, happily. "All ready? Come on."

So they went.

At first Pooh and Rabbit and Piglet walked together, and Tigger **ran round them** in **circles**.  Then, when the path got narrower, Rabbit, Piglet and Pooh walked one after another, and Tigger ran round them in oblongs.

When the gorse got very prickly, Tigger **ran up and down** in front of them, and sometimes **bounced** into Rabbit. As they got higher, the mist got **thicker**, so Tigger kept disappearing, and then **bouncing** back again. Rabbit nudged Piglet.

"The next time," he said. "Tell Pooh."

"The next what?" said Pooh. Tigger appeared, **bounced** into Rabbit and disappeared again.

"Now!" said Rabbit.

He jumped into a hollow
and Pooh and Piglet
jumped in after him.

The Forest was **silent**.

They could see nothing and hear nothing.

Then they heard
Tigger pattering
about.

"Hallo?"

he said.

Then they
heard him
pattering
off again.

They waited a little longer and then Rabbit got up.

"Well!" he said, proudly. "Just as I said! Come on, let's go!"
They all **hurried off**, with Rabbit leading the way.

"Why are we going along here?" said Pooh.

"Because it's **the way home!**" said Rabbit.

"I *think* it's more to the right," said Piglet, nervously.

They went on. "Here we are," said Rabbit, ten minutes later. "No, we're not . . ."

"It's a funny thing," said Rabbit, another ten minutes later, "how everything looks the same in a mist. Lucky we know the Forest so well, or we might get lost."

Piglet sidled up to Pooh from behind.

"Pooh!" he whispered.

"Yes, Piglet?"

"Nothing," said Piglet, taking Pooh's paw. "I just wanted to be sure of you."

When Tigger had finished **waiting** for the others to catch him up, and they hadn't, he decided he would go home. Kanga gave him a basket and sent him off with Roo to collect fir-cones.

Tigger and Roo threw pine cones at each other until they had quite forgotten what they came for. They left the basket under the trees and went back for dinner.

Just as they were finishing dinner, Christopher Robin put his head around the door and asked,

"Where's Pooh?"

Tigger explained what had happened and Christopher Robin realised Pooh, Piglet and Rabbit were lost in the mist on the top of the Forest.

"It's a funny thing about Tiggers," Tigger whispered to Roo, "they never get lost."

"Well," said Christopher Robin to Tigger, "we shall have to go back and find them."

Rabbit, Pooh and Piglet were having a rest in a sandpit. Pooh was **rather tired** of the sandpit, because whichever direction they started in, they always ended up at it again.

"Well," said Rabbit after a while. "We'd better get on. Which way shall we try?"

"How about we leave," said Pooh, "and as soon as we're out of sight of the sandpit, we try to find it again?"

"What's the good of that?" asked Rabbit.

"Well," said Pooh, "we keep looking for Home and not finding it, so if we looked for this pit, we'd be sure not to find it, and we might find **something** we *weren't* looking for, which might be just what we were looking for **really**."

"Try," said Piglet to Rabbit, suddenly. "We'll wait here for you."

Rabbit walked into the mist. After Pooh and Piglet had waited twenty minutes for him, Pooh got up.

"Let's go home, Piglet," he said. "There are twelve pots of honey in my cupboard, and they've been calling to me for hours. I couldn't hear them because Rabbit would talk, but if nobody is saying anything then I shall know where they are. Come on."

They walked off together. For a long time Piglet said nothing, then suddenly he made a squeaky noise because now he began to know where he was. Just when he was getting sure, there was a shout and out of the mist came Christopher Robin.

"Oh! There you are," said Christopher Robin carelessly, trying to pretend he hadn't been anxious.

"Here we are," said Pooh.

"Where's Rabbit?" asked Christopher Robin.

"I don't know," said Pooh.

"Oh well, I expect Tigger will find him. He's sort of looking for you all," said Christopher Robin.

"Well," said Pooh, "I've got to go home for *something* and so has Piglet, because we haven't had it yet, and . . ."

"I'll come and watch you," said Christopher Robin.

So he went home with Pooh and watched him for

some time.

All the time Christopher Robin was watching Pooh, Tigger was tearing around the Forest making loud yapping noises for Rabbit. And at last, a very Small and Sorry Rabbit heard him. And the Small and Sorry Rabbit rushed through the mist at the noise, and it suddenly turned into Tigger:

a Friendly Tigger,

a Grand Tigger,

a Large and Helpful Tigger,

a Tigger who bounced, if he bounced at all, in just the beautiful way a Tigger ought to bounce.

"Oh, Tigger, I am glad to see you," cried Rabbit.

Piglet Does a Very Grand Thing

One windy autumn morning, Pooh and Piglet were sitting in their Thoughtful Spot.

"What I think," said Pooh, "is we'll go to Pooh Corner and see Eeyore. In fact, let's go and see everybody."

Piglet thought they ought to have a Reason
for seeing everybody if Pooh could think of
something. Pooh could.

"We'll go because it's Thursday," he said. "We'll
wish everybody a Very Happy Thursday."

By the time they got to **Kanga's house** they were so **buffeted** by the wind that they stayed to **lunch**.

It seemed rather cold outside afterwards, so they pushed on quickly to **Rabbit's**. "We've come to wish you a **Very Happy Thursday**," said Pooh.

"Oh I thought you'd really come about something," Rabbit said. They sat down for a little . . . and by-and-by Pooh and Piglet went on again.

Christopher Robin was so glad to see them that they stayed until very nearly tea time, and had a **Very Nearly** tea. Then they hurried on to Pooh Corner, to see Eeyore before it was too late to have a **Proper Tea** with Owl.

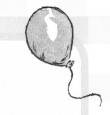

"Hallo, Eeyore. We came to see how your house was," said Piglet. "Look, Pooh, it's still standing!"

"I know," said Eeyore.

"Well, we're **very glad** to see you, Eeyore, and now we're going on to see Owl," said Pooh.

"Goodbye," said Eeyore. "Mind you don't get **blown away**, little Piglet."

The **wind**

was against

them now,

and Piglet's ears **streamed**

out behind him like banners.

It seemed like hours

before he got them

into the shelter

of The Hundred

Acre Wood.

In a little while they were knocking and ringing

cheerfully at **Owl's door**.

"Hallo, Owl," said Pooh. "I hope we're not too late

for . . . I mean, how are you, Owl?"

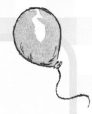

"Sit down," said Owl, kindly. "Make yourselves comfortable." They made themselves as comfortable as they could.

"Am I right in supposing that it is a very **Blusterous day** outside?" Owl said.

"Very," said Piglet, who was quietly **thawing** his ears.

"I thought so," said Owl. "It was on just such a **Blusterous day** that my Uncle Robert, a portrait of whom you see upon the wall . . . What's that?" There was a **loud cracking noise.**

"Look out!" cried Pooh. "Piglet, I'm falling on you!" The room was slowly **tilting upwards**. The clock **slithered along** the mantelpiece, collecting vases on the way, until they all **crashed** together on to what had once been the floor, but was now trying to see what it looked like as a wall.

For a little while it became **difficult** to remember which was really the north. Then there was another **loud crack** . . . and there was **silence.**

In the corner of the room,
the table cloth wrapped
itself into a ball
and **rolled** across
the room.

It **jumped** up
and down and
put out two ears.

Then it **unwound**
itself, revealing
Piglet.

"Pooh," said Piglet, nervously. "Are we still in Owl's house?"

"I think so."

"Oh!" said Piglet. "Well, did Owl always have a letterbox in his ceiling? Look!"

"I can't," said Pooh. "I'm face downwards under something, and that, Piglet, is a very bad position for looking at ceilings."

Owl and Piglet **pulled** at the chair and in a little

while Pooh came out.

"What are we going to do, Pooh?" asked Piglet.

"Well, I *had* just thought of **something**," said Pooh.

And he began to sing:

I lay on my chest
And I thought it best
To pretend I was having an evening rest;

I lay on my tum
And I tried to hum
But nothing particular seemed to come.

My face was flat
On the floor, and that
Is all very well for an acrobat;

But it doesn't seem fair
To a Friendly Bear
To stiffen him out with a basket-chair.

And a sort of sqoze
Which grows and grows
Is not too nice for his poor old nose,
And a sort of squch
Is much too much
For his neck and his mouth
and his ears and such.

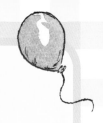

Owl coughed and said that if Pooh was sure that was all, they could now give their minds to the **Problem of Escape**.

"Could you **fly up** to the letterbox with Piglet on your back?" Pooh asked.

"No," said Piglet, quickly. "He couldn't."

Pooh's mind went back to the day when he had **saved Piglet** from the **flood**, and everybody had **admired him** so much. **Suddenly**, just as it had come before, an **idea** came to him.

"I have thought of something," said Pooh. "We tie a piece of string to Piglet. Owl flies up to the letterbox, with the other end in his beak, pushes it through the wire and brings it down to the floor. We pull hard at this end, and Piglet goes slowly up at the other end."

"And there he is," said Owl. "If the string doesn't break."

"Supposing it does?" asked Piglet.

"It won't break," whispered Pooh comfortingly, "because you're a Small Animal, and I'll stand underneath, and if you save us all, it will be a Very Grand Thing to talk about afterwards."

Piglet felt **much better**, and when he found himself going up to the ceiling, he was **so proud** that he would have called out 'Look at me!' if he hadn't been **afraid** that Pooh and Owl would let go of their end of the string to look at him.

Soon it was over.

Piglet

opened

the letterbox

and **climbed**

out.

He turned to squeak

a **last message** to

the prisoners.

"It's all right," he called. "Your tree is blown
right over, Owl, and there's a branch across the door.
I will be back in about half an hour with Christopher
Robin. Goodbye, Pooh!" And without waiting to hear Pooh's
answering, "Goodbye and thank you," he was off.

"Half an hour," said Owl. "That will just give me time to **finish that story** I was telling you about my Uncle Robert – a portrait of whom you see **underneath you.** Now let me see, where was I? Oh, yes. It was on just such a **Blusterous day** as this that my Uncle Robert . . ."

Pooh closed his eyes.

A Poem about Pooh

Pooh is a Silly Old Bear
Who lives life without a care.
He's happiest when he has honey,
The taste of it makes him go funny,
Goloptious honey, sticky and runny!

That clever Bear of Little Brain,
Saved Piglet from the pouring rain!
There's nothing that he wouldn't do,
Life is fun with friends like you.

The Best Bear in All the World – Pooh!

A Poem about Eeyore

Eeyore is old, he's grey and he's slow,
He may, if you're lucky, nod a hello,
But he's probably pondering a sad reflection
And thinking with gloom of his sorry dejection.

Eeyore eats thistles, and wonders "Why?"
He may, if you're lucky, look up with a sigh,
But mostly his low expectations are such
That he's grateful to any who think of him much.

A Poem about Tigger

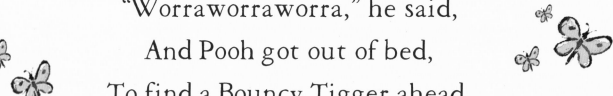

He came to the Forest late one night,
The noise was enough to give Pooh a fright.
"Worraworraworra," he said,
And Pooh got out of bed,
To find a Bouncy Tigger ahead.

Tigger now lives with Kanga and Roo,
Eating enough Medicine for two!
Never was an animal bouncier than he,
(Except when he was stuck up a tree.)

A Friendlier Tigger there never will be!

A Poem about Piglet

Piglet is Small
But that's not all:
His bravery shows
That when the wind blows
His dear friends mean more than ever before
As he battles his way through a bluster.

So what does he do?

With persuasion from Pooh,
He climbs up some string
(What a Very Grand Thing),
To go and fetch help (not so much as a yelp)
And save his dear friends from a fluster.

Good bye.